EVERY SCOOP OF LIGHT

A Story About Repairing the World

Written by Ilene Cooper   Illustrated by Omer Hoffmann

Abrams Books for Young Readers
New York

God was Everything.

But being Everywhere and Everything could be lonely.

What to do?
God decided to create some room,
and a piece of Everywhere became empty.
God knew just how to fill this vast, open space.

Soon enough, there was land and seas, skies and stars.

Then came plants

and animals,

BAA

and finally . . .

People!

All kinds of people—all colors, all shapes and sizes.
God loved the way people were different.

"I will send them gifts. Special gifts," God decided. "I will send all the best things that are a part of me. Happiness and health. Wisdom and kindness. Love and laughter. Celebration and imagination. Peace. Serene, soothing peace."

God was thrilled to have thought of so many
wonderful things to send to the people.
Reaching into the heavens, God took scoops
of light and covered the gifts with their glow.

God was in a hurry to send the gifts on their way and quickly slapped clay vessels in shape to hold them.

In went happiness and health, brightly shining. Wisdom and kindness politely followed one another as they were dropped inside a jar, while love and laughter hugged and giggled.

Imagination and celebration excitedly jiggled next to each other, trying to find room. Peace calmed the others with its hopeful presence.

With a giant whoosh of breath, God sent the vessels on their way.

Then something awful happened!

As the clay jars flew down from the skies, they began to crack. The closer they came to Earth, the shaky-er and break-ier they became.

God had intended the gifts to have soft landings around the world. Instead, the hastily made jars shattered as they fell to the ground. And worse, the precious gifts they held scattered, their lights dimmed.

Bits of happiness and health floated in the wind.

Kindness got lodged under rocks,

while wisdom hid among the scrolls in the library.

Imagination and celebration got tangled in the trees, and love drifted out to sea.

Laughter flew about
finding it all very funny.

Peace was so fragmented it almost disappeared,
made thinner and thinner by rain and snow.

God, looking down, was sad. And mad that such a wonderful plan
had gone awry. "Why didn't I take more care with the vessels?"
God fretted. "What a waste of such precious gifts!"

Then an idea began to form. God excitedly called out,
"People, people, gather. I have something to tell you!"

The sound of God's voice surrounded the world.
People could hear it reverberate inside and outside themselves,
glorious and astonishing. The people came closer.

God told them about the gifts that had been sent—and what had
gone wrong. "I need your help," God said.

Everyone, young and old, big and small, looked at each other. How could *they* help God?

Why did God even need their help?

"You must find all the bits and pieces," God said with excitement. "Every scrap of happiness. Each giggle of laughter. All the words of wisdom and everything else."

A child timidly asked, "Where should we look? And how will we know when we find your gifts?"

God beamed at the child. "Look everywhere! Search with your heart, and it will tell you when you've found something dear and important. Oh, you'll know."

Since the child had been bold enough to speak, a woman stepped forward and asked, "But God, what are we supposed to do with all these bits and pieces when we find them?"

"Work together putting them right. Then share them!" God said.

"Laughing is much more fun when a friend—or a stranger—is laughing with you.

Wisdom makes you smarter when you teach what you've learned to someone else.

Love isn't love unless you share it."

The people began whispering to one
another. They began to see how they
could make the world more wonderful.

Then a man climbed on a rock where God could see him. "This seems like an awful lot of work," he said, frowning. "Why can't you just fix it all yourself?"

God considered this. "I could, I suppose."

The man turned to the others. "See, God just wants us to do all the work. Why should we?"

Then he faced God. "Why should we?"

God was silent for a moment. Then the answer came.

"Because this is your world as much as it is mine. Maybe more. You should be a part of making the world better. Fixing it is a big job. It won't be easy, and it won't be quick, but it will be worth it. Will you do your part? Will you help?"

So the big, beautiful job began.
It is still going on to this very day.

And God smiles.

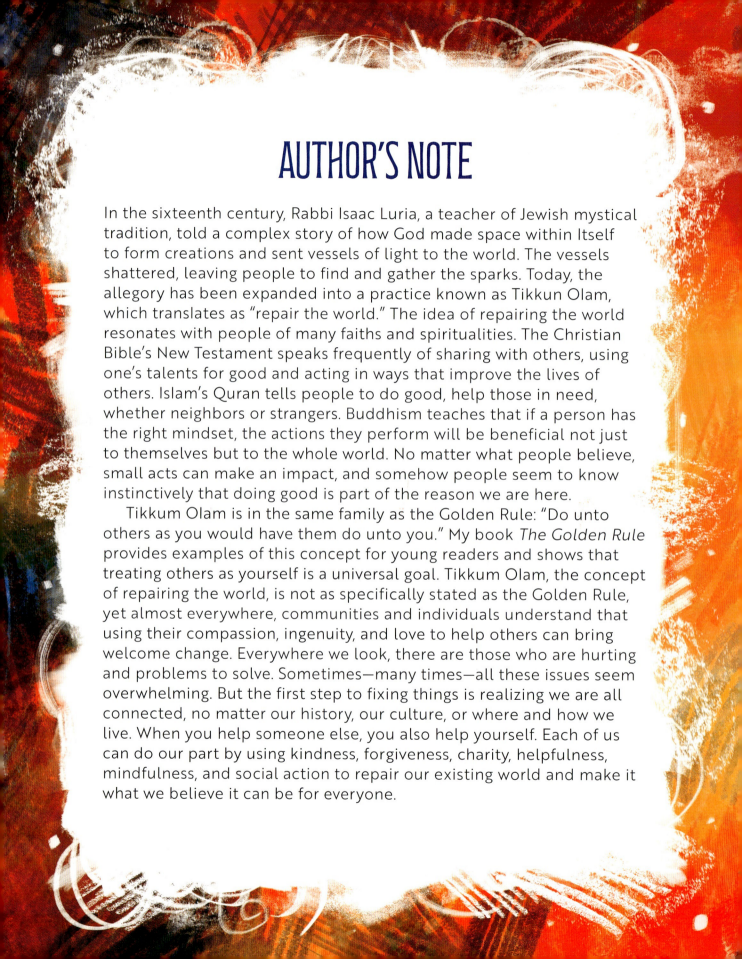

AUTHOR'S NOTE

In the sixteenth century, Rabbi Isaac Luria, a teacher of Jewish mystical tradition, told a complex story of how God made space within Itself to form creations and sent vessels of light to the world. The vessels shattered, leaving people to find and gather the sparks. Today, the allegory has been expanded into a practice known as Tikkun Olam, which translates as "repair the world." The idea of repairing the world resonates with people of many faiths and spiritualities. The Christian Bible's New Testament speaks frequently of sharing with others, using one's talents for good and acting in ways that improve the lives of others. Islam's Quran tells people to do good, help those in need, whether neighbors or strangers. Buddhism teaches that if a person has the right mindset, the actions they perform will be beneficial not just to themselves but to the whole world. No matter what people believe, small acts can make an impact, and somehow people seem to know instinctively that doing good is part of the reason we are here.

Tikkum Olam is in the same family as the Golden Rule: "Do unto others as you would have them do unto you." My book *The Golden Rule* provides examples of this concept for young readers and shows that treating others as yourself is a universal goal. Tikkum Olam, the concept of repairing the world, is not as specifically stated as the Golden Rule, yet almost everywhere, communities and individuals understand that using their compassion, ingenuity, and love to help others can bring welcome change. Everywhere we look, there are those who are hurting and problems to solve. Sometimes—many times—all these issues seem overwhelming. But the first step to fixing things is realizing we are all connected, no matter our history, our culture, or where and how we live. When you help someone else, you also help yourself. Each of us can do our part by using kindness, forgiveness, charity, helpfulness, mindfulness, and social action to repair our existing world and make it what we believe it can be for everyone.

ARTIST'S NOTE

Illustrating a tale set in ancient times can be a lot of fun. I had the opportunity to sketch a diverse array of vibrant fashions, typically outside my usual repertoire, all showcased by people from various cultures. I also got to dive headfirst into the world of archeological references—statues, paintings, engravings, pottery, and much more. I could never get bored!

At the same time, it proved to be quite a task.

It all boiled down to my initial decision—to be as inclusive as I can. A reader should feel that his or her world is represented in a picture book whose theme is humanity as a whole. Therefore, I set myself on a path: illustrate a tale that takes place in ancient times and include as many of humanity's ancient cultures as I could.

However, I had to define WHAT is considered ancient. Is ancient something that occurred 2000 years ago? 3000? Or maybe 6000? The problem was a lot of the cultures I wanted to include just didn't exist at the same time, since they developed or evolved during different eras. While a few cultures coexisted, such as Egyptians and Canaanites (they even painted each other!), most lived millennia apart. For instance, ancient Sumerians lived some 7000 years ago, while ancient Greeks lived "only" 3000 years ago.

The problems didn't stop there, as geography also proved an issue. Unfortunately for me, plenty of nations weren't neighbors. For instance, ancient Chinese did not meet Mesoamericans. Time and entire oceans conspired against me in order to separate ancient people! Should I not only go against history but bridge—literally—the geographical gap as well?

 To make some sense of this situation, I had to take some creative freedom and make sweeping decisions. First, I treated ancient times as a flexible term. Most of the old world I would draw would be between 6000 and 1500 BC. Secondly, since I wanted to include cultures from across the globe, exceptions had to be made for cultures dating up to 500 BC, or as old as the references I could find, in order to include nations from all over the globe. In this book, diversity and cultural representation are more important than historical accuracy.

 Don't treat this story as a history book; treat it as the wonderful, humane fable that it is. And I hope the fun and humor will make up for the historical mishmash.

FOR MY BROTHER, HARVEY. AND FOR THE FRIENDS
AND FAMILY WHO HELPED REPAIR MY WORLD
—I.C.

TO LENNY AND ZOE, MY TWO TRUE GIFTS
—O.H.

The illustrations in this book were created with a combination of pencil, charcoal, and brush and ink, assembled digitally in Photoshop.

Cataloging-in-Publication Data has been applied for and may be obtained from the Library of Congress.

ISBN 978-1-4197-6421-9
eISBN 978-1-64700-812-3

Text © 2025 Ilene Cooper
Illustrations © 2025 Omer Hoffmann
Edited by Howard W. Reeves
Book design by Melissa Nelson Greenberg, Jacqueline Conde & Azalea Afendi

Printed and bound in China
10 9 8 7 6 5 4 3 2 1

Abrams Books for Young Readers are available at special discounts when purchased in quantity for premiums and promotions as well as fundraising or educational use. Special editions can also be created to specification. For details, contact specialsales@abramsbooks.com or the address below.

Abrams® is a registered trademark of Harry N. Abrams, Inc.

ABRAMS The Art of Books
195 Broadway, New York, NY 10007
abramsbooks.com